THE ORIGINAL SINNERS PULP LIBRARY SAMPLER

TIFFANY REISZ

8TH CIRCLE PRESS • LOUISVILLE, KY

CONTENTS

Praise for the Works of Tiffany Reisz

"Daring, sophisticated, and literary… Exactly what good erotica should be." — **Kitty Thomas on *The Siren***

"Kinky, well-written, hot as hell." — **Little Red Reading Hood on *The Red: An Erotic Fantasy***

"Impossible to stop reading." — **Heroes & Heartbreakers on *The Bourbon Thief***

"Stunning… Transcends genres and will leave readers absolutely breathless." — ***RT Book Reviews* on the Original Sinners series**

"I worship at the altar of Tiffany Reisz!" — ***New York Times* bestselling author Lorelei James**

POKER NIGHT

EXCERPT FROM "THE AUCTION"

You're invited to New York City's hottest dating event: Kingsley Edge's annual King's Trust Charity Auction. New on the auction block this year is Daniel, a wealthy widower and dominant. However, he happens to have his eyes on another first-timer in the club's auction: Anya, a strikingly beautiful virgin submissive from his native Canada. Now let the bidding begin...

The
Auction

D aniel could barely breathe from the shock. Eleanor…naked…kneeling on his bed and grinning at him like the last eighteen months had been the setup to a bad joke, and finally, here she was to deliver the punchline.

He slid across the bed and took her into his arms. "You…what are you doing here?" He held her tight to his chest, stroked her hair, her back.

"You sent me a postcard from Tierra del Fuego. The least I could do is stop in and say, 'Hello.'"

Daniel took her face in his hands. Her eyes shone black as night and her body molded into his.

"Hello." Then he took ownership of her mouth with a kiss so ferocious he knew her lips would be swollen for a day from it. He didn't care. If this is how she returned the favor of a single postcard…he wished he'd sent her a thousand of them.

His hands roamed her body, sliding down her back, grasping her bottom, digging deep into her soft skin. The kiss she returned with equal ferocity as she reached between their bodies to open his pants.

"Are you sure?" he asked, afraid of her answer.

"I'm naked on your bed. Did you think I stopped by for a game of Blackjack?"

"The game is Poker."

Eleanor laughed, and her laughter filled the

room, the apartment, the building, the whole city, and even his heart that for so long had sat empty.

Weaving his fingers through her hair, he kissed her again. And again. He couldn't get enough of her mouth, the taste of her lips, the tease of her tongue against his.

"I can't believe you're here," he breathed into her ear and, while there, bit her earlobe.

"I heard your laugh on the stairs. I don't know how, but I knew it was you."

"King wouldn't have given you my address."

Eleanor laughed again, low, throaty, and playfully sinister.

"I beat it out of him."

"What about—" Søren, he tried to say, but she cut him off.

"Are you going to keep giving me the third degree, sir? Or are you going to beat me and fuck me like your life depended on it?"

Breathing in, he inhaled her scent—lilies, orchids—the subtle essence of every hothouse flower he could name graced her skin. She'd always seemed like a hothouse flower—something beautiful and wild yet thrived best in captivity.

If only he could keep her.

"My life does depend on it."

"Well, then..." She slid her hands over his bare shoulders and met his eyes. "Maybe we should stop wasting time."

She pushed his running shorts down and took his hard cock in her hands. Burying his mouth in the crook of her neck, he groaned as the hands he'd dreamed of for a year and a half did everything he remembered they could. With her slim, nimble fingers, she traced the length and width of him, gently caressed the sensitive underside, and cupped his testicles. He groaned with the shameless abandon of a submissive.

"You have to stop, or I'll come in your hands," he warned her.

"Oh, no. Not that. Anything but that." Eleanor pushed him onto his back, and he went willingly. She wrenched his shorts off and threw them against the wall with the flourish of a matador. Then she pushed his legs apart and kissed the inside of his ankle. She kissed the soft indentation right under his quad muscles before dipping her head and biting his inner thigh—hard. Daniel winced. Eleanor only laughed.

Daniel's head fell back as she wrapped her lips around his cock and caressed it with her tongue. With torturously light licks and kisses, she focused her attention solely on the head. As erotic as it was, he needed more than just pleasure. He craved connection. He reached down and found her hand, twined their fingers together.

Real...she was real and warm and here, and God, she was sucking his cock like she missed him as much as he missed her. He knew he'd be fooling himself to believe that. She'd picked Søren over him, and she would probably do it again. Why she was here now, he didn't know, and he didn't care. All he could do was let go and enjoy it.

He let go. With a soft cry and spurt after spurt of come, he filled her mouth. Her throat moved as she swallowed every drop he gave her.

When it was done, Eleanor sat up on her knees and licked her lips. Daniel took her in his arms and pulled her onto him, laying her against his chest.

"I still can't believe you're here."

"I'm here." She smiled blissfully, a little drunkenly. "For now."

"Kingsley said if I agreed to be in his stupid auction, he'd let me see you again."

"You got conned. King doesn't get to decide who I see and don't see."

"But Søren does."

"If you really believe that, you don't know me very well."

Daniel laughed softly. "Here I thought you were the world's greatest submissive. Turns out, you're the world's greatest actress."

"I really am a terrible submissive. I submit when I want to, not when he wants me to. Which is fine with him. According to him, it's more fun to punish me when I deserve it."

"You always deserve it."

She turned her face up to his, grinned, and Daniel kissed her, tasting himself on her lips. The mix of his salt and her sweetness set his blood to boiling again. Pushing her onto her back, he pinned her wrists to the bed.

"I know you'll go back to him tonight." Daniel dipped his head and lightly sucked on each nipple before kissing his way back to the hollow of her throat, "but you'll take my bruises with you."

Helpless underneath him, she panted.

"Yes, sir."

He dragged her from the bed by her wrists and left her standing at the footboard.

"Kneel," he ordered, and she went down onto her knees.

He drank in the sight of her, of this woman he'd longed for day and night for so long. She knelt at the foot of his bed, her back a blank canvas waiting to be painted with welts. From under the bed, he pulled a large case like the ones Kingsley kept in all his townhouse bedrooms.

"Hands on the top rail."

Eleanor reached up and grasped the top of the metal footboard.

Daniel stood behind her as he handcuffed her wrists to the railing.

"I have very fond memories of this bed," he told her as he pushed her hair off her back. "Maggie and I bought it together. She made sure to lay down and test the strength of the footboard and the headboard. The elderly furniture dealer was slightly horrified."

"I wish I'd known Maggie, sir."

"You remind me of her in so many ways." Daniel knelt behind her and kissed the back of her neck and her shoulders. He ran his hand down her side and across her stomach.

Only when he said the words did he realize how true they were. Eleanor's spirit, her sense of humor, her wild streak that gave him such pleasure to try to tame…so much like Maggie.

"I'll take that as the compliment I know it is, sir."

Daniel didn't answer. Instead, he pressed his lips to the center of her back, kissing the elegant curve of her spine.

He turned his head and bit her, hard, in the center of her back.

She flinched and released a gasp of pain.

"Just marking my target," he whispered in her ear before standing up and grabbing a stiff riding crop from the case.

He counted in his head a full sixty seconds before striking her the first time. She flinched, and the metal of the handcuffs rattled against the metal of the footboard. Music to his ears.

A welt six inches long and the color of fire burned across her pale skin. He struck her again, then again. A fourth time, then a fifth…At ten, she finally broke and cried out. At twelve, he stopped.

He dropped to his knees behind her and pressed his chest to her burning back.

"Did you enjoy that?" he said into her hair.

"Hurt like hell. I loved it."

He reached up and unlocked the cuffs. He knew she'd have to leave sooner or later, and he didn't want to waste a single second with her.

He lifted her off the floor and carried her to the bed. Just to hear that laugh again, he tossed her unceremoniously across the covers. As she was laughing, he grasped her ankles and dragged her hips to the edge of the bed.

No more laughing now.

He went down on his knees for her, spreading her thighs wide and opening her with his fingers. His lips sought her clitoris, and he sucked lightly on it. Her back arched. She pressed harder into his mouth. No woman he'd ever been with tasted quite like her…so sweet and tart at the same time, the scent of her more potent than any drug.

She moaned as he pushed his tongue into her. For the rest of his life, he'd remember the feel of her heels digging into his back and the warmth of her thighs against his face. Still, he couldn't wait any longer. He had to be inside her.

Daniel stood up and lifted her legs over his shoulders as he pushed into her. He wanted to go slow, to savor every second of her. But he couldn't hold back. He thrust into her, hard and deep, savoring the sound of her cry of pleasure.

Eleanor stretched her arms out to each side, and her head fell back in a posture of utter surrender. Daniel slid his hand up her body and took her gently by the throat. Her pulse beat hard under his fingers as he thrust into her again and again.

His fingertips found her clitoris and gently teased it. She responded just as he knew she would, as he remembered she would, grasping at the sheets with desperate fingers, hips lifting, her whole body going stiff for a brief eternity before her inner muscles began to spasm, clamping so hard around him they nearly pushed him out of her.

As Eleanor relaxed under him, Daniel only thrust harder, deeper. He held off as long as he could, not wanting to let go of this moment. She was his, if only for now. She was his, if only while she was under him. He wanted to mark her, write "Mine" all over her body. Since he couldn't, he did the next best thing. He pulled out of her and straddled her hips with his knees. When their eyes locked, he finally came on her stomach.

As the tension slowly drained out of him, Daniel collapsed on top of Eleanor and gathered her to him. He sighed and closed his eyes as she lightly scratched his back. The simple mindless gesture of affection so painfully reminiscent of lovemaking with Maggie nearly did him in. He squeezed his eyes shut tighter and tried to imprint this perfect moment into his mind forever.

"Yes," he said, answering the question she asked an hour ago. "I missed you."

———

THE STORY CONTINUES in The Auction, *available now as an Original Sinners Pulp Library mass-market paperback and ebook from 8th Circle Press.*

THE CASE OF THE SECRET SWITCH

EXCERPT FROM "THE MISTRESS FILES"

Kingsley Edge, The 8th Circle's King of Kink, has instructed his top dominatrix to write down some "best practices" that he can share with the club's other professional dominants. Mistress Nora, who also moonlights as an erotic romance writer, turns his request into a series of sexy shorts For His Eyes Only. The Mistress Files collects five of Mistress Nora's favorite client stories—written in typical Nora fashion in the third person—from Kingsley's files...

THE MISTRESS FILES

The Mistress wouldn't say he was her favorite client, not to his face anyway. When he showed up, she knew he would be the last person she saw that day. He took more out of her than any of the other men who came to her dungeon at the club. He took the most time, the most effort, and he never made an appointment.

Two weeks ago, he came to her dungeon. It had been about three months since their previous session together. It might have taken three weeks for him to heal completely from it. She'd worked him over thoroughly that night, just the way he liked it. The other nine weeks between that night and this one, he'd been too busy to see her, or simply not in the mood to be destroyed. The mood struck him at the oddest times and for seemingly no reason. She never asked him the reasons why he decided to show up at her feet. He wasn't there to talk. He wanted pain, and The Mistress wanted to give it to him.

On a Wednesday afternoon at about four, he strolled into her suite without knocking. The Mistress lay stretched out on the bed reading a book. *Of Human Bondage* by W. Somerset Maugham. A disappointing book. Well-written but she was two hundred pages in, and no one had even been tied up yet. She looked up from her book as he swept in the door, shutting and locking it behind him. He did this often, came into her dungeon. He had every right to. But locking the door meant only one thing.

Play-time.

She didn't speak. She shut the book and tossed it onto the nightstand. From the small table she pulled an elegant black mask that covered only the top half of the face. Like the good and well-trained submissive he was playing that day, he kept his eyes on the floor as she approached him. In all the world, she'd only ever met one man she found more attractive than the one standing before her. Night and day, he and the other man were. The submissive masochist in front of her had olive skin, dark eyes, dark as a sin-stained soul, and black hair with a slight roguish wave that fell to right above his shoulders. And at the moment, he had on far too much clothing.

"Lose the shoes. Shirt, too," she ordered as she slipped the masquerade mask over his eyes. It had eyeholes—she didn't want to blindfold him, only put him in a mental place where he could become another person...someone other than the one who'd walked in her door and the one who would crawl out of it. Plus, no denying, the man looked fucking hot in the mask. With this particular client, she allowed herself to enjoy her attraction to him.

He shucked off his jacket and she took it from him, tossing it on the floor. The embroidered vest came off next. It too landed on the floor. Then the shirt. Raising her hands to his chest, she caressed his strong broad shoulders, his collarbone, the hollow of his throat. She loved to tease him with pleasure before torturing him with pain. With another client who shared his sort of desires and fetishes, she would have put a collar on him. But no, never with him. He had one hard limit, only one: no collars. He was willing to surrender to a world of pain, but drew the line at such an obvious sign of ownership within the kink community.

That didn't mean she wasn't about to treat him like a dog.

"Stay," she said as she went back to the bedside table. She pulled a thin black rope lead from the drawer and returned to him. God, how he hated the lead. Loathed it. The man had pride.

On his own time, maybe. Not on hers.

She leashed it around his neck and slipped the end of the rope through the hole at the other end. It would tighten around his neck if he resisted her. A choke rope. Holding the end of the lead, she took four steps back to stand three feet from him. She tugged once on the lead and he didn't move. Good. She loved it when he gave her an excuse to punish him. Raising her hand she wrapped the rope one time...two times...three times around her palm.

With every turn of her hand, she pulled him closer to her.

"I know you hate this," she said.

"You know me well, Maîtresse."

She yanked him to her so they were eye-to-eye. She wore eight-inch platform stiletto boots that day, otherwise she would have been staring down the center of his chest. Not a bad place to stare. He had a beautiful body, no denying that. Lean and muscular. Riddled with old scars. She wouldn't add any to his vast collection today. Only cuts, welts, and bruises. All injuries that would heal quickly. If he wanted scars, he'd have to pay extra and make an appointment.

"I do know you…but not well enough," she said. "I think I want to get to know you better today. Let's go into my office. Come along."

She gave the rope another yank and led him into the second room of her suite. The front room was the bedroom, which she rarely used with clients. Sexual favors were granted for female clients and lovers only—not male clients. But the second room, the dungeon, housed all her toys. Including her most favorite toy of all.

"Do you know anything about the story of St. Andrew?" she asked as she dragged him by the lead to the ten-foot tall, X-shaped St. Andrew's Cross at the back of the room.

"I'm vaguely familiar with him."

She removed the lead and tossed it aside.

"Up," she ordered and he stepped in front of the cross. "Arms."

He knew the drill well enough she didn't even have to give him the orders. She didn't have to, but she wanted to. She wanted to and he wanted her to. To be brutalized and dominated—that's what he came for. To be dominated and brutalized—that's why he came.

But he wasn't allowed to come yet. He had to earn it first.

She locked his wrists to the bars of the cross and left him standing at the cross while she went to a tiny box and pulled out five silver needle-sharp fingernail extenders. Talons, she called them. How fortuitous that she'd gotten a brand-new set of them this week and sanitized them with fire that very morning.

"So, St. Andrew," she said. "Fun guy. He was Peter's brother, supposedly. *The* Peter—the first pope. They were fishermen, both of them. Brutal profession, catching fish. The rope nets tore up the hands. The work was backbreaking. And imagine how the fish felt—caught in a net, dragged to the surface, drowning in air. They couldn't get free no matter how hard they struggled."

He pulled on the bounds that held him to the cross. "I can sympathize," he said, the lightest hint of amusement in his voice.

"And worse than the net was, of course, the hook."

With those words she pricked his back with her talons. He flinched and five tiny drops of blood appeared on his shoulder like a red constellation.

"That fucking hook," she sighed. "Can you imagine how much it would hurt to have a hook in your mouth? And then to get dragged by that hook all the way to the surface...brutal."

She moved her hand down, and left another five bleeding pinholes in his back.

"We are solitary, poor, nasty, brutish creatures, we humans," he said between winces. "We deserve all the punishment God has to give us."

"I suppose that makes me an instrument of God's wrath, doesn't it? I kind of like the thought of that. Here's a little more wrath for you."

She ran her talons in a straight line down his back, leaving four shallow bleeding rivulets about three inches long. He panted through the pain and she could only smile. With her free hand, she reached around his hip and felt his erection pressing against her hand. Nasty and brutish—his favorite way to play. Luckily, it was hers too.

"Poor St. Andrew...he was crucified too. An X-shaped cross, not T-shaped. He didn't think he was worthy to die on the same sort of cross as his Lord. His brother Peter had already been crucified upside-down. He couldn't go that route either. They got very creative with their crucifying. We might have to get creative one of these days…"

The Mistress let that threat hang in the air as she unbuttoned his trousers. While she stroked him with one hand, her other hand continued to prick his back with tiny pinholes. She'd undergone this particular torture herself a time or two. Bee stings hurt worse but only barely. And at least the bee died after stinging you. No such luck with a sadistic Mistress. She wasn't going anywhere and had nothing but more pain to give him.

"I've always wondered about your love of pain." She ran a finger from the base of his erection to the tip and back down again. "Born masochist? Or made? Nature? Nurture?"

"Who knows? I didn't know I loved it until someone hurt me the first time. After that I couldn't get enough. Was I made? *Peut-etre?* Then again, I didn't know I loved Cabernet Sauvignon until I had my first glass either. But the taste buds, they were already there…"

"I suppose it doesn't matter how you got it. It's here. Drink up." At that, she stroked him hard as she left four more parallel lines of blood on his back.

She removed her talons and sat them aside before stripping her victim completely naked. As she dragged his pants down his legs, she bit his upper thigh, lower thigh, and calf hard enough to leave three black bruises. She couldn't help herself—the man did have exquisite legs.

Now that she had his back bared and bleeding, she decided it might be time to give him some real pain. Of course, she'd broken the skin. That meant a few more precautions would be necessary. She opened a case that had a new deerskin flogger in it—never before used. Doing edge-play with a client meant more work for her during and after. Usually, she charged through the nose for even a cut or two. But for him, well, he was a special case. Not that this was a freebie. To quote The Boss: *No freebies. Ever.*

She stood behind him and examined her handiwork. "You're bleeding," she said. "A lot."

"*Merci,*" was his sole response, the only one she expected, the only one she wanted.

"But they're tiny little cuts. If I left them alone, they'd heal up in two days. Where's the fun in that?"

She raised the flogger and brought it down hard onto his bleeding back. She struck again. And again. She struck high and hard, low and deep. She added welts to the cuts, bruises to the welts. The tips of the flogger tails smeared the blood and soon his entire back had turned a rusty red.

After a good (for her) half-hour of flogging, she dropped the deerskin and let him catch his breath.

"Have you ever safed out with anyone?" she asked as she came to stand at his side again. A few drops of semen had leaked from his cock and she caught them on her fingertip.

"*Non*, Maîtresse."

"You like pain that much? Or is it pride?"

"You know the answer to that already. Why did you never safe out with him?"

"I did," she corrected him. "But only once."

"Why?"

"Because," she said as she wrapped her hand around his erection again and squeezed to the point of pain. "He ordered me to marry him."

"He must be a masochist too," he said through gritted teeth.

The Mistress could only laugh. "Oh, you're gonna get it big time for that."

Big time meant the cane. Not the rattan cane she used to leave the hand-sized bruises on a client's ass or thighs. No, what she needed was the little cane—white plastic, long as a conductor's baton. In fact, it had always reminded her of a baton, one she used to conduct a symphony of pain.

She started under his left shoulder-blade and left a two-inch raised welt by flicking the baton against his skin. An unassuming little toy, no one ever dreamed it hurt as much as it did, not until they felt the fiery force of it. Getting cut with a razor hurt less than this little devil.

"Breathe," she instructed as she flicked it

against him again, barely half an inch below the first welt. "Don't forget to breathe..."

"I'm breathing," he said, although she'd seen him holding his breath seconds earlier. He'd passed out in their sessions, usually during breath-play scenes. No harm, no foul. Fainting, falling, crying, wailing, being hauled to your breaking point and left there staring into the abyss—that's what happened behind locked dungeon doors when the vanilla world wasn't watching and the monsters came out to play. In this room with this man, she had no one to answer to but God, and God wasn't asking any questions right now.

"Good boy. You pass out on me and it's game over. We don't want that, do we? You haven't even come yet. You take thirty more of these," she said, flicking him once more and smiling at the searing red line on his back, "and we'll discuss throwing a little pleasure into this mix."

"Thirty-three welts?"

"What? I like my biblical numbers. Now shut up and breathe." She flicked him again, working her way down his entire left side. By the time she was done with him, there would be no part of his body from his neck to his hip that wasn't either bruised, bleeding, or scoured with welts. He loved his souvenirs, as he called them. Souvenirs from his holidays in Hell.

Up his right side, she decorated him with more welts. To add a little challenge, she made him count the flicks of her baton for the last seventeen strikes.

His "one" sounded strong. The "five" sounded pained. By "ten," he gasped the number. At "thirteen," she could barely hear him.

By seventeen, she'd broken him. It took almost a full minute to get him to say the number.

"I'm waiting…" She ran the baton over his back, letting it tickle his savaged skin. "You want a little pleasure, don't you? If you want a break from the pain, you have to say the number. You know I'll let you hang here all night until you say it. I'll get my book and pull up a chair and read. I have all the time in the world…"

He swallowed hard and shuddered. Poor dear. She'd piled on the pain today on only one part of his body—his back. Usually that much pain she'd spread out over a larger area—back, ass, thighs… Those sorts of niceties she reserved for other clients, however. Gentler clients, weaker clients, tamer clients. But this client got her best because he paid for her best. And when someone paid for her best, she did her worst.

"It's only one more…you can take one more, can't you?"

His only reply was a nod. She saw that behind the mask, he'd closed his eyes, and she took the opportunity to simply take him in.

Who was he? She'd asked herself that question since the day she'd met him when she'd only been sixteen years old. What secrets did he keep behind those eyes and inside that scarred and beautiful body of his? She could have beaten the secrets out of him, but she knew him well enough to know that, in fact, she didn't want to know his every one of his secrets.

"Seventeen," he said in a clear voice, raising up his head.

The seventeenth flick of the baton was the hardest by far. "That was for the 'He must be a masochist' crack."

She kissed his welt before dropping the baton on the floor and breaking it with her foot. She never used a toy on anyone else after she'd used it on him. It was the lone sign of respect she afforded him when he was in submission to her. Once a flogger or cane or blade touched his body, it would never touch another. She either broke it or set it aside to be used in the future on him and only him.

"I deserved that." He relaxed in the bonds, resting his head against his upper arm.

"You did. And worse. I'm trying to decide how much worse."

"I will submit to anything you desire, Maîtresse."

"I know you will. That's the problem. Too many choices. I could cane your legs. I could pour some scalding candle-wax on your testicles. Hmm...So many ways to make you my bitch. Hard to choose just one."

"Are you open to suggestion, Maîtresse?"

He turned his head and peered at her through the space between his arm and the cross. Of course, they both knew he shouldn't be making eye contact with her. This evening, she was in charge, she was the Dominant, and he was nothing but property for her to use and abuse any way she wanted. But she had trouble being angry at him for something as human as looking in her eyes. How would she see his hunger, his need, his humble desperation if she didn't see his eyes? She'd give him a pass on the eye contact this time. She'd only flog him a little more. Nothing vicious. She'd save the viciousness for the next time he did it.

"And what, pray tell, is your suggestion?"

His only answer was to laugh, and the laugh was all she needed to hear. A low throaty masculine insinuating thigh-melting, knee-shivering panties suddenly disappear and end up hanging off the bedpost sort of laugh. Glad to know he wasn't the only one in the mood.

"Well, it is a good suggestion."

"*Merci,* Maîtresse."

"If I'm going to do it, you're going to have to earn it."

"I understand," he said, almost solemnly. Nothing like a threat of having to "earn it" could put the fear of God back into a sub. She'd already ripped his back apart in three different ways. Time to give the front side The Mistress treatment.

She unlocked his wrists from the cross and turned him around, slamming his back roughly into the painted wood. He flinched visibly as his back made contact with the cross. He'd be in agony for a week at least after today. Maybe two.

As she buckled his wrists to the cross, she felt his erection pressing against her stomach. Nothing got him harder than pain. Not threesomes, not orgies, not dominating, not submitting, not anything. She knew his need for release was so strong now it had become yet another form of torture. Good.

"You're dying to come, aren't you?" she asked as she pushed her hip into him, sending him into shudders.

"Death would be a relief right now."

"I won't let you die. That would be too merciful. I'm not really in the mood to be merciful today. I am, however, in the mood to redecorate. You know I love your scars, the bullet wounds, all of them...but I think you could use some new designs here." She ran her hand all over his chest. "Nothing permanent. Wait here." With a light and insulting slap-tap on his cheek, she sauntered off. She returned with a Wartenberg wheel and her violet wand.

"Now I know you don't play with violet

wands, and that's fine. But I do. And the reason I do is because they can make such wonderful patterns on skin when used the right way. Or the wrong way. However you want to think of it."

"You're a sadist," he said, his head leaning back against the cross. He looked up as if to seek help from the heavens. Help, unsurprisingly, did not come.

"Flattery will get you everywhere."

She plugged in the wand and held the contact in one hand and the Wartenberg pinwheel in the other. The electricity didn't affect her as she'd made herself merely a conduit. Sparks buzzed from the sharp tips of the wheel, and with a slow and steady pace, she rolled it in a straight line down the center of his chest. He inhaled sharply as the electrified wheel left a thin raised line on his skin. She'd been on the receiving end of this technique before. The wheel never broke the skin, but the combination of electricity and sharp edges made the recipient feel like he was being sliced open.

"Only five lines, I think," she said. "Count them for me. That was..."

"One..." he panted.

She ran the wheel down his chest a second time, then a third. She ran it over the old scars, over his nipples, across the sensitive skin of his lower stomach. When she touched his hipbone with it, he coughed from the pain. He had to say the "five" twice because of how labored his breathing had become.

"Was that five already? Very good."

He exhaled heavily in noticeable relief.

"But let's do one more set. In French. Say 'un,'" she ordered and ran the wheel once more down his chest.

The sound that escaped his throat was more animal than human. Exactly what she wanted to hear.

By the time they reached *cinq,* he had ten criss-crossing lines on his chest, thin and red as a brand. The welts would fade fairly quickly. The ones produced by the wheel and the wand wouldn't last more than a day or two. Amazing that something that felt like one's chest being cut open by a knife could cause no lasting harm at all.

"On a scale of one to ten," she asked him as she put the wand away and tossed the wheel into the trash can, "what was that?"

"*Onze,*" he said, his eyes closed tight as his whole body shivered from the last aftershocks of the pain.

"*Onze?* I hurt you all the way to eleven? I'm pretty damn proud of myself right now, I have to say." She brought her lips to his chest and licked one of the lines from tip to tip. Her hot mouth against his seared skin must have felt like salt in an open wound. And yet he'd only grown more aroused from this latest round of agony.

Perhaps it was time to put him out of his misery.

———

THE STORY CONTINUES in The Mistress Files, *available now in a new Original Sinners Pulp Library mass-market paperback edition and ebook from 8th Circle Press.*

TRAINING DAY

EXCERPT FROM "SUBMIT TO DESIRE"

Charlotte Brand is tired of dull boyfriends and boring sex. Kingsley Edge, who owns clubs rumored to supply more than just cocktails, seems just the man to revive her: intense, sophisticated...and looking for a submissive he can train for an elite client. Soon, they are engaged in a series of lessons that test her darkest desires...

SUBMIT
TO
DESIRE

"Your lovers have been vanilla," Kingsley said. "That's a tragedy. Did you even enjoy fucking them?"

Charlotte shrugged her shoulders. "They were nice. I had orgasms. It wasn't terrible. Just—"

"Boring? Unfulfilling? Bourgeois?"

"All of that, I guess. Simon told me I was crazy to keep dumping such great guys. He said he'd take them if I didn't want them."

Kingsley took Charlotte's wrists and tied them high to the bedpost. Water from her shower ran down her back and her legs all the way to her ankles. The water droplets itched and tickled but she couldn't reach down to wipe them off.

"You would have been crazy to stay with men who didn't understand you. Compromise is one thing. Denying your true self is another. Now..." He stood behind her. "I'm going to do something to you that is neither boring nor bourgeois. I'm going to flog you for five minutes. And if you make it through those five minutes without saying your safe word, I'll give you an orgasm. And then I will flog you for eight minutes. And then I will give you another orgasm. And so on and so on. I'll add three minutes to each beating. And the game only ends when you safe out."

"What if I don't safe out?"

"Then we'll be here for a very long time," he

whispered into her ear. "Because there's nothing in the world I enjoy more than beating a beautiful woman and then bringing her to climax. Now where did I put that cat?"

"Cat? You have a cat?"

"Cat of nine tails, Charlie. Now be a good girl and just stay put while I find a few things."

Charlotte was fairly certain Kingsley knew exactly where everything was. He just wanted to leave her tied up naked and waiting, letting the anticipation scare her. She heard what sounded like a trunk opening and then she felt him standing behind her again. Something landed on the bed. It was brown leather with a six-inch handle and nine leather thongs. It didn't look terrifying. But it didn't look fun, either. Something else landed on the bed—a tube of lubricant. One more thud—a rather impressive-looking vibrator. She blinked as Kingsley brought his hand around and waved a stopwatch in front of her face.

"Five minutes." He set the alarm. "Ready?"

"Yes, sir."

"You're trying to get me to fuck you by calling me 'sir,' aren't you? It will work. But not yet."

Before she could say anything else, the flogger was off the bed and he'd landed the first blow on her back. She flinched at the sudden burning pain. It was shockingly sharp, but not unbearable. She breathed through her nose in short desperate bursts. She was determined to not to say her safe word. It wasn't so much that she wanted the orgasm. She wanted to prove to Kingsley she wasn't boring.

When she heard the chiming of the stop-watch alarm she sagged with relief. Kingsley pressed his bare chest into her burning back. The flogger landed on his bed again.

"Did you enjoy that, Charlie?"

"No," she said, still panting.

"Good. I hate beating masochists. They take the fun out of it by actually enjoying the pain."

"I'm letting you do this to me," she said between breaths. "I'm not a masochist?"

"Oh, no, Charlie. You're not a masochist. You're a slut."

"I am not—"

He hushed her before she could finish her angry protest.

"Charlie, in this house, the word *slut* is the highest compliment I can give. It means you are a person who owns her sexuality and is unafraid to experiment and open her mind and body to new experiences. I'm a slut, too."

"I've noticed."

"Now that you've had your pain, I suppose you'll be wanting your pleasure."

Kingsley reached out for the lubricant and opened the tube. He slid his hand between her legs and applied a generous dose to her labia. She shivered from the cold and the wet, but relished the pleasure his dexterous fingers were giving her.

"I know I was a little rough on you last night. But I can be merciful."

He took the vibrator and turned it on. He moved Charlotte's legs apart and slid it slowly into her. She inhaled as it went deep inside her. Her body slowly stretched to take it all in.

"This is merciful?" she asked.

"It's not as big as I am."

He moved it in and out of her slowly as his fingers found her clitoris and teased it. The vibrator did its work quickly. She cried out as her body spasmed around it and against Kingsley's hand. He pulled it out of her and laid it on the bed again.

"I'll give you another one in eight minutes," he whispered into her ear. Again he set the alarm on the stopwatch. Her body was still twitching with pleasure when the flogger struck her sore back. She concentrated on her waning pleasure and tried to ignore the growing pain.

She found that if she opened her back instead of clenching her muscles, the agony was flatter, less acute. Her head fell back. She stared up at the ceiling. After a few minutes she barely felt anything at all.

A chiming sound jarred her from her trance.

Kingsley picked up the vibrator again and pressed the tip against her clitoris. She gasped from the shock of pleasure. She'd never been with a man who understood how to manipulate a woman's body so well. The pressure on her clitoris was perfect. His fingers inside her found all her sensitive spots. He seemed far more concerned with her orgasms than his. She couldn't believe what she thinking. She was tied to a bedpost for a flogging and all she could think about was how good he made her feel.

Charlotte's orgasm spiked into her stomach and she almost wrenched her shoulder from how hard she flinched.

"If you can take eleven minutes of beating, then I'll fuck you again," Kingsley whispered into her ear. "How does that sound?"

"Very good."

Kingsley slapped her hard on her right thigh.

"I mean, very good, sir."

———

THE STORY CONTINUES in Immersed In Pleasure/Submit To Desire, *available now in a new Original Sinners Pulp Library mass-market paperback edition and ebook from 8th Circle Press.*

BIG BRAD WOLFE

EXCERPT FROM "LITTLE RED RIDING CROP"

Mistress Nora needs a vacation. She might be the one flogging the clients, but Kingsley, her sexy French boss, is the real sadist who rarely gives her a day off. They strike a backseat deal: Nora gets a month-long trip to Europe if she can sneak into a rival BDSM club and get the dirt on the owner. But Nora will need more than her little red riding crop when she comes face to face with Brad Wolfe, the one man who stands between her and freedom...

LITTLE
RED
RIDING
CROP

T he heels of her boots echoed hollowly off the wet concrete and the sound followed her to the green door at the entrance to Black Forest.

A rare case of nerves overtook Mistress Nora. She'd beaten the shit out of some of the biggest, toughest men in the world if they paid her enough for the privilege. But they'd wanted her to, invited her to. Here at Black Forest, she came unwanted, uninvited—on a clandestine mission for her boss, Kingsley Edge.

Not only that, but Black Forest had the biggest damn Dom in all of Manhattan. To comfort herself, she took her red riding crop out of her toy bag and held it by the handle. One never knew...

Nora tried the doorknob and found it locked. No worries there. She started to open her toy bag to dig out her lock-pick set when the door flew open so suddenly she gasped.

The man said nothing, asked no questions, and made no introductions. Of course, he didn't need to say anything or make any introductions. Nora knew Brad, had seen him before, had met him before...but no matter how many times she'd seen him she could never wrap her mind around the sheer size of the man. At six foot four he stood no taller than her tallest ex-lover. But where most tall men tended toward the lean side, Brad was muscle from shoulder to shoulder, neck to ankle, and so wickedly handsome with his lupine smile and his salt and pepper hair that Nora could never look at him without wanting to get hip to hip.

Enemy, she reminded herself sternly. *No fraternizing with the enemy.*

"Shouldn't you be at the gym?" Nora said, recovering her composure quickly. "I can see you shrinking by the second."

"Well..." he said looking Nora up and down. He seemed to take particular note of what she held in her hand and her red cloak. "If it isn't Little Red Riding Crop."

Nora gave him her brightest, broadest, most obnoxious smile. "If it isn't the Big Brad Wolfe. We meet again."

"And me not even properly dressed." Brad wore nothing but a pair of loose-fitting black pants and a black shirt...unbuttoned.

"I have that same shirt." Nora tapped her chin. "Well, actually it's a bed sheet. Same size. Very comfy."

"I've heard tales of your bed, Mistress. Urban legends."

"I live in Connecticut. They'd have to be suburban legends. I've heard tell of your bed too. Trees for bedposts, right?"

"You're getting me confused with Odysseus."

Nora raised an eyebrow, impressed despite herself. "Brawn and brains—I would never have guessed. But then again, I don't know anything about you."

"Born in Albany. Played football at Rutgers. Rhodes scholar. Love kink. Hate normal jobs. Divorced. No kids. There. That's the beginning and end of my life story."

"Divorced, huh? Vanilla ex-wife?"

"How'd you guess?"

"I'm smart too. Used to a fuck a Rhodes scholar. By the way...are you going to invite me in?"

"Should I?"

Nora thought about that question and decided honesty would win her more points than charm.

"Nope."

Brad raised a dark eyebrow at her and said nothing. Maybe she should have gone with charm.

While waiting for Brad to make up his mind, Nora started to twirl her riding crop in her hand like a baton. She did that often when burning off nervous energy.

Brad merely watched her. How many staring contests with gorgeous men was she going to get into today?

"If I let you in, will you promise not to break anything...or anyone?" Nora spun the crop one more time.

"Nope."

"The Dame will have my hide if I let you in and you know it."

"Then let's hope you're into that sort of thing."

Nora smiled again at him, the smile she reserved for midnight conversations whispered across black sheets. It seemed to work. Brad took a step back and let her pass.

Finally inside Black Forest, Nora took a moment to simply look around. Kingsley's Underground Empire included half a dozen clubs all over Manhattan. But he only had one club that existed solely for their kind. The 8th Circle, as it was known to insiders, had been carved from the ruins of an old condemned hotel. Kingsley hadn't done much to spruce up the joint. The seediness of the club suited the clientele. But where The 8th Circle quietly catered to money, Black Forest reeked of it. Black chandeliers with black light bulbs swung low from the black and gold ceiling. Leather chairs and sofas littered the floor. A dozen doors lined the first and second levels—doors that led to private rooms for secret activities.

"You don't like it, do you?" Brad came to stand behind her so close she could feel the heat of his skin radiating from his bare chest.

"Bit middle-class, isn't it? Got a Rotary Club feel to it."

"It's a helluva lot nicer than that shit-hole you work in."

"Exactly. We don't have to look pretty to get

our millionaires through the door. They get that at home."

"Black Forest is doing extremely well."

"Must not be doing that well if you have to keep poaching Kingsley's people." Nora spun around and attempted to stare Brad down. It would have worked but she had to look too far up to stare him down.

"Kingsley works his people into the ground. No days off. No breaks. No vacations."

"He's a sadist."

"He's a bad boss."

"And The Dame is so much better?"

"She is actually."

"Then I should meet her," Nora said, heading toward the stairs. "We can talk 401Ks and dental insurance. You get dental, right?"

For a man built like a linebacker, Brad could move with shocking speed. He interposed himself between Nora and the staircase and stared down at her.

"That's not fair." Nora flashed him a frown. "If I can't stare you down you can't stare me down."

"You're on The Dame's territory. She makes the rules. I enforce them."

"Great plan. I'd like to talk to her about it." Nora tried to push her way past Brad and got nothing for her trouble but a few delicious seconds with her hand on his chest.

"No one talks to The Dame."

"Then I'll just listen."

"No one listens to The Dame either."

"Fantastic boss you have there then. Come on, Brad. Five minutes. All I need is five minutes with her."

"For what? Are you really thinking of leaving Kingsley for this middle-class Rotary club, as you called it?"

"I don't know. Maybe. Let me talk to The Dame. If she makes me an offer I can't refuse...well, then I won't refuse it."

"I do the recruiting for the club."

"Well then..." Nora took a step back and tapped her chin with the tip of her riding crop. She saw something heated and mischievous gleaming in Brad's dark eyes. "Maybe you should try to recruit me."

"I have Mistress Irena now along with four other Dominatrixes plus three male Dominants, including me. We're not hiring any more Doms."

"Pity. I have an impressive resume. And a huge client list. Everyone's on it."

"Everyone?"

"Your dad's on it."

Brad burst out laughing, and Nora only waited, her eyes wide with feigned innocence.

"You should be punished for bringing my father into this discussion," Brad said, raising a hand to her face. Nora didn't pull away. He might slap her. He might pinch her nose. He might even kiss her. She wouldn't have objected to any or all of those possibilities.

But instead of a slap or a pinch or a kiss, he simply caressed her cheek with his thumb. She started at the gentleness, the intimacy of the touch, and took a step back.

"What was that for?" she demanded, raising a hand to her face. The caress burned more than a slap would have.

"You're beautiful."

"And you're huge and handsome. You don't see me going around getting all personal with your face."

"Would you like to get personal with my face?"

"I..." Nora stopped and swallowed. She needed to get back into control of this situation. She could handle Brad. She could handle any man. Well, except for one... "You're trying to top me, aren't you?"

"I told you. We're all stocked up on Domina-trixes. What we really need are a few good subs."

Nora's spine stiffened. "I don't sub."

"Not anymore, right?"

Nora glared at him.

"Come on, Nora. Everyone knows who you used to belong to. It's not a secret."

"Not a secret, no. But not anything I want to talk about."

"Was it all that bad, being a sub for him?"

Nora let her most dangerous smile spread across her face. "No. It was that good."

"Then you should enjoy doing it again."

"You're a big man, Brad, but not even you could fill his shoes."

"Worth a shot, isn't it? You want to meet The Dame, then you have to get through me."

"Through you? Or under you?"

"Both."

———

THE STORY CONTINUES in Little Red Riding Crop, *available Fall 2021 in a new Original Sinners Pulp Library mass-market paperback edition from 8th Circle Press. The ebook edition (without the bonus content and new cover) is available now.*

FATHOMS

EXCERPT FROM "IMMERSED IN PLEASURE"

The Manhattan Mermaids—all of whom are virgins—entertain wealthy, powerful men in an exclusive club called Fathoms. Derek Prince doesn't believe they really exist, until he meets the stunningly sensual Xenia...

IMMERSED IN
PLEASURE

"I'm telling you, Guys, they're mythical creatures. They're like, I don't know…unicorns or mermaids," Christian said.

At the mention of mermaids, Derek started paying attention to the conversation again. For the last five minutes as Mark and Christian discussed their women troubles—specifically how many ex-boyfriends their current girlfriends had—Derek tuned them out and stared at an empty table across the nightclub.

"They are real actually." Derek raised his Old-Fashioned to his lips. "I knew one once."

"A virgin?" Mark asked. "A virgin over the age of twenty-one? I don't buy it. They don't exist."

Derek smiled into his drink.

"Yes, she was a virgin," Derek said. "And a mermaid."

"Bullshit." Christian threw his napkin at Derek.

"No, he means it." Mark leaned back and gave Derek a long look. "Plus, he's the pretty one. If any of us were going to bag a virgin mermaid, it would be Derek Prince."

Derek half-laughed and rubbed his forehead. She'd called him pretty too. God, had it really been a whole year? He reached into his pocket and pulled something out. He didn't show it to Mark and Christian, merely held it in the palm of his hand before tucking it into his pocket again.

"Believe it or not, it's true. And I saw her first right over there..."

Derek pointed to the table he'd been staring at earlier.

"Over there?" Christian asked, a notice of real concern in his voice. "At the VIP table? Kingsley Edge's table?"

Kingsley Edge, a wealthy half-French businessman of both renown and ill-repute, owned Cirque du Nuit, the club Derek, Mark, and Christian frequented at least once a week. According to rumor, catacombs resided under Cirque du Nuit, catacombs that started under the club and stretched out into New York City like underground tentacles. Legend had it that all of Kingsley Edge's various clubs could be reached through the catacombs.

"Didn't know that then," Derek said. "It was a year ago. I was waiting for Ireland to show up—"

"Dude, I'm so glad you got rid of her," Mark interjected.

"And I saw this girl," Derek continued and felt his mind leaving the present and swimming back into the past. "This amazing girl with wet hair."

At his first glance of the girl he thought she was one of those women who went bat-shit crazy with the hair-gel. But when she moved her hair moved with her. Not hair gel, just water. The white camisole she wore reached only to the bottom of her ribcage and had gone nearly transparent from the water in her hair. When she stepped into the blue light, he could just make out her pale pink nipples under the fabric. That alone would have held his attention all night except for one thing—she wasn't just wet and wearing transparent clothes, she was beautiful. Her dark brown hair hung in dripping ringlets over her face and down her back. She looked young, maybe only twenty or twenty-one, too young for this club anyway. Her large dark eyes and light-olive skin sported no makeup that he could discern. Watching her, he noticed she moved uneasily. A noise came from the edge of the club and she flinched, her eyes flashing wide open like a startled animal's. Twisting her hands in her hands she seemed uncomfortable in her surroundings and utterly out of her element.

Derek hadn't been able to take his eyes off her. Other than her little white camisole she wore a white skirt that rested low on her hips and revealed the full expanse of her flat stomach and lower back. The skirt clung tightly around her slim legs all the way to her ankles.

She must have sensed his stare because she turned his direction and stared back. Derek knew he shouldn't be staring, that he must seem like a psycho to her. But the stare she returned wasn't angry, only inquisitive. Cocking her head to the side like a curious cat, she watched him watch her.

"So she was wearing all white and was wet from head to toe?" Christian asked.

Derek nodded. "I know. Sounds crazy, right? Gets crazier."

"What happened?"

"My table caught on fire," Derek said. "She saved me."

A man of about thirty-five with dark hair pulled back into a roguish ponytail sat with the girl. He wore a dark grey Victorian-era suit and riding boots. Derek rarely noticed other men but he couldn't deny that the unusually handsome man the wet-haired girl sat with had an aura of power and mystery about him. The man snapped his fingers and the girl immediately turned her head to the sound. She drew close to him and the man whispered something in her ear.

Smiling, the girl pulled away. Derek's stomach tightened as she left the VIP area and walked gingerly down the steps headed toward his table. In her skintight skirt she came to him, her steps nervous and delicate. As she walked he noticed for the first time that she wore no shoes.

"Hello," Derek said as she sat across from him.

The girl stared at him for a moment.

"Your table's on fire," she said. Derek tried to discern if she was joking. He saw nothing in her eyes but innocent sincerity.

"What?"

She pointed at his centerpiece. A black candle and a blue rose decorated every table in the club. His rose had dipped its head too near the flame and now quietly smoldered.

"Holy shit." Looking around wildly, he started to reach for his glass but it contained an Old-Fashioned. Alcohol plus fire equaled a nightclub in ashes.

The girl laughed a soft tinkling laugh. Slowly she rose and leaned over the table. Taking her long brown hair into her hands, she twisted it, wringing just enough water out to douse the burning rose.

Because he didn't know what else to do, he laughed.

"I'm glad this club has such gorgeous firemen on duty."

She ran her hands through her wet hair and separated it into three sections.

"I'm not a fireman." She hummed as she braided her long hair with nimble fingers.

"What are you then?"

"I'm a mermaid."

She stretched out her leg toward him. Derek didn't know what he was supposed to be looking at but then he saw them. At first he thought her feet sported silver foot jewelry of some kind. But no, metallic silver tattoos of fins adorned the tops of her small, pale feet.

"No way," Mark interrupted. "She was one of *those* mermaids?"

"She was," Derek said, taking a sip of his drink. "I didn't think they were real either. Not until that night."

The Manhattan Mermaids. Believed to be the most beautiful women in the city, they entertained the wealthiest, most powerful men in the world. Kingsley Edge didn't just own Cirque du Nuit. He owned four or five other clubs, some of them so secretive they didn't even have names. One of the most exclusive was known as Fathoms. Fathoms supposedly had the usual sort of chic-chic nightclub stuff—cocktail waitresses, ridiculously opulent decor. But in addition to that, Fathoms had one thing no other club in the city had—mermaids. One could tell a mermaid if you met her on the street by two things, Derek had heard—they wore little silver mermaid pendants around their necks, and they had silver and blue metallic tattoos on their feet and ankles. Derek looked the girl up and down —check and check.

"You're a real mermaid?"

She gave him a mischievous grin.

"Come find out."

Just then Ireland decided to make her appearance—an hour late. For almost the entire hour he'd been desperate for her to show up. Now that he saw her breezing through the door and heading his way, he fervently wished he'd been stood up.

"I can't," he said.

The tiniest glint of disappointment shone in the girl's midnight blue eyes. In such an open innocent face, the sadness rebuked him. He felt as if he'd knocked a baseball through a stained-glass window.

"Then goodbye," she sighed. "I'll never see you again."

She said the words with such earnestness that Derek knew he would be the idiot of the century to miss this chance. It wasn't only that The Manhattan Mermaids were so legendary he still couldn't quite believe he'd been talking to one. It was her—this girl—not the rumors and legends who'd gotten to him. She'd saved his life...or at the very least his centerpiece. And she had such innocence about her. He didn't meet innocent people in his line of work. As a defense attorney he was often called a shark. Briefly he wondered if sharks and mermaids were natural enemies or allies.

As Ireland reached the table, Derek made up his mind.

"You're late," he said.

"Couldn't remember if we were meeting at nine or ten," she said, shrugging. He couldn't recall just then why they were dating. Brainy and beautiful with her white-blond hair and her legs that went on for eternity, Ireland, unlike his ex-wife, was fantastic in bed and wasn't afraid to try anything. But she was also cold and arrogant when she wanted to be. Tonight she apparently wanted to be. "Guess it was nine."

"Let's make it eleven. We'll meet at your place at eleven and then I'll be an hour late." He stood up. "See you at midnight."

"Wait, where the hell are you going?" Ireland demanded. "I just got here."

"And I'm just leaving."

Derek raced to the VIP table and found it depressingly empty. His mermaid and the dark-haired man had vanished. The only sign the girl had even been there was a small puddle of water on the floor by the chair she'd been sitting in.

Water…Derek stopped looking around and started looking down. Not far from the VIP table he found the watery outline of a bare footprint on the floor. A few feet later he saw another tiny puddle of water glinting on the shiny dark blue tile. The drops led to a door tucked in a corner.

A metal EMPLOYEES ONLY sign decorated the door and gave Derek pause. In a club owned by Kingsley Edge, breaking the rules led to unpleasant consequences. But he'd abandoned one of the sexiest women in New York at his table for this chance, and he wasn't going to miss it.

He threw open the door and found a stairwell. Racing down the stairs, he prayed the water on the floor had come from her and not some clumsy waitress. At the landing two levels below Cirque du Nuit he knew he was on the right track. Breathing in, he inhaled warm wet air scented with a trace of chlorine. He passed through another door and stopped immediately when he discovered he wasn't in Cirque du Nuit anymore or even the club's basement.

He was in Fathoms—no doubt about it. And Fathoms sat right below Cirque du Nuit. Looking around the dimly lit club, Derek couldn't believe the legend was true. The underground catacombs did connect all of Kingsley Edge's clubs.

Derek hid behind a column and studied his surroundings. The club had dozens of interconnected swimming pools scattered about the large room. Between and about them sat tables and chairs—chairs occupied by the highest of high society. Derek recognized several faces— with a real estate mogul for a mother and the deputy mayor for a father, Derek could recognize the wealthy and famous on sight. And everywhere he looked he spied money and power.

At the center of the room stood a two-story high transparent column about twelve feet across. In it swam a girl completely naked but for a silver belly chain. The silver fins tattooed on her feet, ankles and thighs glinted in the light. He tore his eyes from the column to another corner of the room. Another girl equally beautiful and equally naked, sat on a large rock at the edge of one of the pools. A man Derek recognized as a city councilman said something to the girl. She rolled her eyes and splashed water in his face. The gesture made the man laugh as if it was some sort of honor to be splashed by such a woman.

Derek tore his eyes from the scene and searched the club for his mermaid. Looking up, he saw a metal walkway at the top of the large column and a flash of white skirt. He found a staircase behind him, and at the top of the staircase he came suddenly face to face with his mermaid.

"Hello," she said, standing in a private alcove next to the top of the central swimming pool. "I thought I would never see you again."

"I forgot to thank you for putting out my fire," he said, wincing at how stupid he sounded.

She ran her fingers through her hair freeing it from its braid.

"I'm waiting," she said, humming.

"For what?"

"For you to thank me. You said you forgot to."

Derek shook his head.

"Right. Thank you for putting out my fire. I didn't mean to stare at you upstairs. I've never seen a mermaid before."

"I stared back," she said simply.

"You did. Why?"

"I like your face."

"You like my face?"

"I do. It's pretty. But not girl pretty. Handsome prince pretty. And you have hair that's wavy like water. Even your eyes are water-colored, and your shirt. I probably thought you were a merman."

Derek looked down. He wore black slacks and a black vest over his French blue Oxford shirt. A little too GQ for him, he only wore these clothes because Ireland liked them so much.

"I'm not a merman. But I am a prince. Derek Prince," he said and held out his hand to her.

"Xenia." She ignored his hand and instead leaned forward to kiss him on the cheek. He shivered as her warm soft lips pressed into his cheek. "I have to go now, but you can stay if you like."

"Go where?"

"Underwater."

At that Xenia took a step back and pulled her camisole off. Her skirt came off next, and she stood before him completely naked.

Derek felt his eyes go as wide as hers. Although a sight to behold, the club paled before

Xenia's naked flesh. Thin but with soft girlish curves, Xenia barely looked human to him. The silver metallic scale tattoos graced not only her feet and calves but the sides of her thighs and the edge of her hips. Her breasts, the perfect size, appeared designed to rest in the palm of his hand. A healthy red-blooded man, he couldn't help but stare at her breasts and between her legs. Completely smooth and hairless she seemed a being of eternal youth. His body tensed at the sight of such pristine flesh so unashamedly on display.

The girl, Xenia, reached for a silver chain and fastened it around her stomach. Little silver scales hung off it and dangled around her hips. She clasped silver bracelets on each wrist and connected them to the silver rings on her fingers. Around her forehead went a heavier silver chain like a small circlet. The body jewelry shimmered in the low light and rendered Xenia a creature of ethereal beauty.

She strode to the edge of the tall pool and dove gracefully into it. Derek ran back down the stairs and up to the side of the column. Around and around she swam, her long brown hair flowing behind her. She spun in slow graceful circles, arched under and around, and seemed to need almost no air. Derek watched her unable to look at anything else. She swam to the edge of the column and smiled at him through the water. He pressed his hand to the glass and she laid her hand against the inside to meet his. But she pulled back quickly and swam off again....

———

THE STORY CONTINUES in Immersed In Pleasure/Submit To Desire, *available now in a new Original Sinners Pulp Library mass-market paperback edition and ebook from 8th Circle Press.*

CANDY AND MISCHIEF
EXCERPT FROM "MISCHIEF"

When Mistress Nora's young submissive lover Nico admits he's always wanted to celebrate a real American Halloween, she summons him to Halloween Town, USA—a.k.a. Salem, Massachusetts—for two nights of nothing but candy, sex, and mischief. If necessary, they can skip the candy...

MISCHIEF

Nora took Nico by the hand and led him into the bedroom. She already had the gas log fireplace burning and the lights turned low. This was a short trip and Nora didn't want to waste a single second.

"Need anything before I tie you to this bed and leave you there for about an hour?" she asked him.

"Only you." He bent to kiss her again and during the kiss he untied the sash of her robe. He delicately stroked her sides and back with his fingertips, and the tickling sensation through the silk was utterly delicious.

"Did you miss me?" she said. "It's been forever since we saw each other."

"Six weeks," he said. "Longer than forever."

Nora had spent a part of August and September with Nico at his vineyard, playing chatelaine. By day, she wrote, read, and helped Nico with his vines. By night, she taught Nico how to serve her. She loved the days with him almost as much as the nights. That's how she knew it was real love, even if it had complicated her life a little bit more than she'd bargained for...

"We'll make it a good two nights," she said as she touched his lips. Beautiful lips, soon to be swollen from bites and kisses.

"Good already," he said, bending to kiss her again. "Perfect already."

She didn't let him kiss her this time. Instead

she stepped back to tease him and he narrowed his eyes at her in playful frustration.

She sat in the large leather club chair with a seat wide enough it could have fit two of her. She threw her bare legs over the chair arm and waved her hand at him, indicating he should undress for her viewing pleasure.

Nora could tell Nico was trying not to smile and/or roll his eyes as he removed his black jacket, folded it in half, and dropped it on the ottoman. He wore a plain white V-neck t-shirt underneath, which he pulled off without fuss or fanfare.

"You'd make a terrible male stripper," she said, even as she admired his lovely strong chest, his lovely stronger shoulders and arms.

He knelt to take off his shoes. "I can't dance either."

"My poor moosh," she said, using her favorite pet name for him. He'd told her his grandmother always called him that as a child since he was so quiet. Moosh meant "mouse" in Farsi. "It's okay. I didn't fall in love with you because of your stripping or dancing skills."

"Why did you fall in love with me?" he asked. He stood up and kicked off his jeans. Nora looked at his tight, toned twenty-six-year-old naked body.

Then she looked at it again.

"A few reasons."

She stood up and walked to him, pressed a

kiss to his bicep and breathed in the warm scent of his sun-kissed skin. When he reached for her she danced out of his reach again.

"Ah, you drive me crazy," he said.

"That's my job. Lie down on the bed on your back. Think happy thoughts."

"I am," he said. She wrapped her fingers around his erection and stroked it upward.

"I can tell."

With a put-upon sigh, the sort Frenchmen were best at, he crawled onto the bed. He lay in the center, face up. Nora dug through her toy bag until she found the wrist and ankle cuffs she'd bought specifically to use on Nico. They were the softest, most supple leather she could find, ten times the price of any cuffs she ever used on her clients.

But Nico was hers, and he was special and it gave her enormous pleasure spoiling him even if he didn't realize she was doing it. Though his vineyard was a success and he made plenty of money, he invested it all back into the company and rarely bought anything extravagant for himself. He and Kingsley were nothing alike in that regard. Kingsley had spent years being driven around in a Rolls Royce. Meanwhile, Nico drove a twenty-year-old Land Rover and had seen a Rolls Royce once. In a movie.

Before Nora wrapped the cuffs around Nico's ankles, she massaged his calves and feet for a few minutes. The feet were a personal part of the body, vulnerable. Very few people ever had their feet touched by anyone but a masseuse or pedicurist. She liked touching Nico's feet to remind him that she owned all of his body, even the most vulnerable parts. Especially the most vulnerable parts.

Nico's breath hitched as Nora rubbed his arches with her knuckles. It always took him a few minutes to get acclimated to being treated like a possession whenever they reunited. Unlike her, he had no other lovers when they were apart, nor did he want any, he'd said. He liked his quiet life. He liked his privacy. He liked giving all of himself to his vines and his wine. It took some getting used to, he confessed, to be touched again by someone other than himself. But those moments of rediscovery, of being touched again for the first time after weeks alone, he'd said, were like the first bite of an apple in autumn after a long season of waiting for them to ripen. The first might be so tart it would set your teeth and make your cheeks ache. Yet nothing in the world could stop him from taking that second bite.

That he said things like that to her without shame or embarrassment was one of the reasons she'd fallen in love with him.

Nora buckled the cuff around his right ankle. Nico closed his eyes while she buckled the cuff around his left.

"You enjoy this?" she asked.

He nodded. "Who wouldn't?"

"Fools," she said. "Fools and madmen. And dominants, which are the same thing."

"You're a dominant," he reminded her.

"Yes, which is how I know."

Nico laughed softly at her, one of her favorite sounds in the world and the perfect accompaniment to cuffing his ankles to a spreader bar. She threaded rope through the ends of the bar and tied it to the bedposts, leaving Nico's legs locked open about two feet apart at the ankles. There wasn't much more in the world Nora liked looking at more than Nico tied to a bed. However, the main reason she cuffed him was because it was difficult for him to just lay there and let her service him sexually when all his instincts told him he should be the one servicing her.

They were good instincts. Usually she encouraged them. But when she wanted to play with him like a pussy with a moosh.

Nora slid onto the bed and straddled Nico at his waist. Immediately his arms were around her, pulling her down to him.

"This is why I have to cuff you," she said as he ran his fingers through her hair, caressed her face and neck. "You're handsy."

"How could I not be? You're beautiful. But if you want me to stop..." He dropped his hands over his head on the pillow.

"Why are you such a good submissive?" she

asked, smiling down at her beautiful boy. "Hmm? Any ideas?"

"When Rembrandt says he wants to paint your portrait, you sit down and you hold still and you say thank you to the master for picking you out of the crowd," Nico said. "That's why."

Nora wagged her finger at him. "You…you are a silver-tongued devil."

He shook his head no, and stuck his tongue out at her. It was pink, just like hers.

"Put that tongue back in my mouth where it belongs," she said before kissing him again. The kiss grew so heated so quickly that Nico forgot himself again and wrapped his arms around her.

Without warning, she rose up onto her knees, grabbed him by the wrists, and slammed them over his head into the bed. She used her full weight to hold him down and enough pressure to leave two thumbprint bruises on the sides of his arms. He inhaled sharply at the pain and went still. It wasn't often Nora showed off around Nico. She didn't have to. He was her lover, not a client, and he adored her whether she did whip tricks for him or not. But every now and then she liked to remind him what she did in her other day job.

"You like that?" she asked.

He replied with a single word: "Rembrandt."

"Just for that," she said, "I'm going to be very nice to you right now. Ready?"

He nodded.

Nora released his wrists to fetch the cuffs and the rope. When he was strapped to the bed and unable to lift his hands, she reached back into her bag of tricks and pulled out a treat.

"For my moosh," she said. "A kiss."

And it was a kiss. A Hershey's Kiss. Dark chocolate—her favorite kind. She set it in the hollow of Nico's throat.

"I can't eat it like that," he said.

"You're not going to eat it. Not yet. You're going to lie there while I ride your cock into this bed. If you move so much it falls out, then you don't get to come tonight. And if you manage to hold still enough while I use your cock to make myself come, then you get to come. And then you get your treat."

"You're a sadist."

"You asked for candy and mischief," she said. "And that's exactly what you're going to get."

———

THE STORY CONTINUES IN MISCHIEF, *available now in a new Original Sinners Pulp Library massmarket paperback and ebook edition from 8th Circle Press.*

SCARS AND STRIPES

EXCERPT FROM "THE LAST GOOD KNIGHT"

It's lust at first sight when Mistress Nora encounters a sexy newcomer to The 8th Circle. She's happy for the distraction, since she left her lover, but her session with Lance is cut short when her boss, Kingsley Edge, reveals they're all in danger...

THE
LAST
GOOD
KNIGHT

"I can do it. Try it again." Nora took a deep breath followed by a deeper drink of her vodka and tonic.

"Mistress, this is the fourth time." Simone gave her a pleading look. "Are you sure?"

"I'm sure. I got it this time. I'm ready. Do it, sub. Go."

"Okay, okay." Simone ran a hand through her rainbow-colored hair and looked Nora in the eyes. "How old are you?"

Nora stared at Simone without blinking. "I am..."

"You can do it, Mistress."

The ice in Nora's glass rattled in her hand.

"Thirty."

"Holy shit!" Simone applauded. She threw her arms around Nora and gave her a kiss on the cheek. "Good job!"

"Oh, my God, that was hard." Nora rubbed her temples. "I hate being thirty. I swear I was in my twenties a week ago."

"You *were* in your twenties a week ago."

"That explains it. Thank you, Rainbow Slut. I needed a little help getting to stage five in the grieving process."

"Stage five?"

"Acceptance."

"Happy to help you find acceptance any-time, Mistress." Simone leaned against Nora's shoulder, and Nora kissed her on top of her multicolored hair. With or without rainbow-striped hair, Simone would have been attractive, but no one could miss that mass of soft, flowing hair that fell down her back in an array of five different bright colors.

"What the hell do you use on your hair, anyway? Kool-Aid?"

Simone giggled and Nora decided she had probably earned a beating tonight. Simone looked up at her with eager eyes and the Mistress pressed a long kiss onto her carmine-colored lips. Maybe the rainbow-hued sub had earned more than a beating.

"If you ask nicely, I might beat you *and* fuck you," Nora said against Simone's lips. Simone groaned, but not in an erotic way.

"I can't, Mistress. I'm booked." Simone looked heartbroken, devastated and miserable. And utterly adorable.

"Who booked you? I'll kill him."

Simone shrugged and shook her head. "I don't know. Mr. King told me I was needed in the bar at ten, which is—"

"Now," came a familiar voice from behind Nora. She didn't turn around. She didn't need to. She'd know that cold, pretentious, overeducated voice anywhere. "Simone, shall we?"

"Yes, Mr. S.," Simone said, and Nora could tell she was trying not to smile—not in front of the Mistress anyway. The only person Simone enjoyed subbing for more than Nora was Søren, and Søren was her ten o'clock. Well, wasn't that just peachy.

"Eleanor…" Søren said and Nora refused to turn around and look at him.

"Søren. Have a lovely evening."

"I certainly plan to. Excuse us."

Simone shot Nora a final apologetic glance as she took Søren's proffered arm like a lady with her squire. No one could play the part of the gentleman better than Søren, but it was all an act. She and Simone knew that from personal experience. When he shut the dungeon door behind him, the gentleman turned into a sadist and all pretense of chivalry died. Thank God. Søren was no gentleman and she was no lady. And that's how it should be down here.

Out of the corner of her eye, she watched Simone disappear from The 8TH Circle's VIP bar. She kept her eyes lowered respectfully, her posture submissive, but Nora saw the pleasure of anticipation gleaming in her eyes. By day, Simone worked on her Ph.D. in International Relations. She paid for that expensive education with money earned on the floor and in the dungeons of Kingsley's S&M clubs. But Simone never charged Søren a penny for his hour with her. With Søren it was always pleasure, never business. Nora knew that Simone and almost every other submissive at the Circle would pay *him* for the privilege of a beating. And to think once upon a time, Nora belonged to him—

heart, body and soul. And she'd given it up for this. For freedom.

And it was worth it. At least that's what Nora told herself.

Nora spun on the barstool and gazed round the club. A quiet night, as weeknights usually were. Quiet*er*, anyway. Only two hundred or so deviants floating about instead of the usual five hundred on Friday and Saturday nights. But this was a school night. Half the members of the club were married and had kids. At least 90 percent of her clientele were married men who'd rather lie to their wives and come to Nora to explore their fetishes than tell the truth to the women they'd pledged to love and honor. It was a good thing, too. If the wives of the world were a little more open-minded about male submission and fetishes, where would she be?

Out of a job.

Feeling frustrated by Simone's abrupt departure, Nora took another drink of her vodka. Maybe she should call it a night, go home, get some sleep. She might even get up early tomorrow and work on her new book. Kingsley didn't let her have much in the way of free time these days, now that her career as a Dominatrix had taken off. In two years she'd become the go-to gal for all things kink. The money poured in. The pain poured out. Days off were few and far between.

As she hopped off her stool, the elevator at

the end of the bar rose. Maybe Kingsley had decided to come up for air finally. She hoped so. She wanted to chew him out for sending Simone to Søren when Nora had already decided that Simone would belong to her tonight. Not that Kingsley had known that, but Nora never missed any opportunity to drive Kingsley halfway up the wall. Maybe she'd make him take Simone's place on her St. Andrew's Cross tonight.

But no, it wasn't Kingsley who stepped out of the elevator. It was a different man—one she'd never seen before. He wore black jeans and black boots, a red T-shirt stretched over his broad chest. He had a good tan, short dark hair and a handsome face—handsome in a rugged sort of way with half a day's stubble and troubled eyes. Troubled? Interesting. *Nervous* she might have expected, especially since he seemed to be new. But troubled? That was a mystery she had to solve.

The man came up to the bar and ordered a boring American beer. With nonexistent effort he popped the top off and drank it in a few easy swallows. She noticed a handkerchief tucked in his back pocket—black on white: a submissive looking for a Dominant. This evening was starting to look up.

"Military," she said, walking over to the bar stool next to him. "Am I right?"

"Is it the haircut?" he asked.

"And the really good posture. Let me guess... Army Ranger. All you guys are kinky fuckers."

He laughed a little.

"I'm insulted."

"Oh, insulted, are you? Gotta be a Marine, then."

He shook his head. "Keep guessing."

"That's 'Keep guessing, *Mistress*' to you."

He swiveled on his stool and for the first time looked straight at her. She wore black thigh-high boots decorated with a dozen silver buckles, a red leather skirt, red corset, black jacket and a black top hat complete with red band. She looked amazing and she knew it. Kingsley had gotten the best tailor in the city to design her fetish wardrobe. Yet another reason she'd been looking for a little play tonight. Shame to waste such a good outfit on an evening of celibacy.

"Keep guessing, Mistress." He bowed his head in deference.

"Only one type of military more proud of themselves than the marines. Navy SEAL?"

He said nothing. Only sipped at his beer.

"I knew it. SEAL," she said. "Give me a second to pat myself on the back."

She reached her arm around her shoulder and swatted herself awkwardly.

"This is harder than it looks," she said. "Don't laugh at me." Nora switched arms and tried patting herself from around and behind her back. "I'm going to keep doing this until you admit you're a SEAL."

She crossed her arms over her face and then stretched back to pat herself again. Her breasts nearly popped out of her corset.

He laughed even harder.

"Fine. Just stop that before you hurt yourself," he said, a broad grin taking over his face and a twinkle shining in his dark blue eyes.

Nora immediately dropped her arms to her sides.

"Whew. Thank you. That was getting weird fast."

"For both of us."

"What are you doing at my club, Mr. Navy SEAL? I know it's not Fleet Week. I have Fleet Week marked on my calendar. And my underwear."

"It's Mr. Ex-Navy SEAL. And I'm here because I was told to come tour the place, enjoy myself and see if I liked it."

"You do like it, don't you?" Nora rested her chin on her hand and waggled her eyebrows at him.

"It's definitely…entertaining?" He turned the word into a question. She didn't blame him. Hard to find the right word to describe The 8th Circle. Most days she just called it home. "Nice floor show."

"I'll be here all week." Nora held out her hand. "I'm Mistress Nora. Nice to beat you."

Instead of shaking her hand, he took it delicately and brought it to his lips for a kiss.

"An honor to serve you, Mistress Nora. I'm Lance."

"Would you like to serve me, Lance? I haven't been served all week." She gave him a wide smile, a smile with a promise, a promise she fully intended to keep.

"Someone should serve a woman like you every single day, or as often as you desire, of course."

She took her top hat off and set it on the bar. Without pretense or shame she perused his body. One good thing about being a Dominatrix—she got to have as much fun as the men of this world did. Dominatrixes weren't just *allowed* to treat men like sexual objects, they were expected to. Hell, they were even paid to. Down here the Dominatrixes were treated like queens. Even the male Dominants usually gave them wide berth. Every male Dominant except for a certain arrogant six foot four blond she'd like to see on her cross one of these days. Kink or crucifixion, either one worked for her.

"You're good at this," she said, impressed by his attitude.

Lance leaned in a few inches and lowered his voice.

"I've had a little practice, Mistress."

The Mistress raised her chin.

"Only a little? You need a lot more practice than that. Wanna go practice?"

"We just met."

"Are you calling me a slut because I asked you to play?" She batted her eyelashes at him.

"No, ma'am. Never." His laugh reached all the way to his dark blue eyes. She loved a man who could laugh.

"Am I calling *you* a slut by asking you to play?"

"You can call me anything you want."

The Mistress placed a hand on Lance's thigh and felt the hard muscle under the denim.

"You looked troubled when you came in here. And your entire body is tense. I'd like to flatter myself that you're hard all over because of me, but you looked uncomfortable before you saw me. What's up?"

Lance nodded at the bartender who brought him another beer.

"I haven't played in a long time. I'm not even sure if I should be here."

"Should you be here? Or did you sneak in?"

"I just got a job working for Kingsley Edge."

"Never heard of him." Nora kept a straight face. Kingsley tried to keep employees from fraternizing with each other too much, a hopeless cause where Nora was concerned. Lance must be the new house manager he'd hired. It would take someone with a military background to keep Kingsley's coterie under control.

"He's some rich kinky bigwig. Owns this place. Club membership is one of the fringe benefits."

"You like it here?"

"I feel a little out of place. My first time in a club like this."

"A club full of rich and famous perverts?"

"Exactly. I'm neither. Well, not the rich and famous part, anyway. Pervert maybe. This is definitely not my usual crowd."

A congressman on the leash of a Domme crawled on all fours past the bar.

"Don't worry. They're not my crowd, either. Don't be intimidated." She leaned forward and crossed her legs. "I'll let you in on a secret. The top Dominant here is a Jesuit priest, and he comes here in his clerical collar all the time. Jesuits take a vow of poverty. Everyone defers to him even though he's not rich. He earned that respect. No one has ever ratted him out."

"That's a comfort, Mistress. Nice to feel safe."

"You are safe down here. And you're with me. I'll protect you from the rich and famous perverts."

"My hero," he said, turning toward her so that their lips were only an inch apart.

"Come on, Lance," she whispered. "Come play with me. Submit to me. You know you want to. I know you want to. You're not on duty right now, are you?"

"No." He shook his head. She could see him trying to bite back a smile.

She moved her hand from his thigh to his crotch and felt his erection.

Lance closed his eyes and inhaled sharply.

"What do you want to do, Sailor?"

"Anything you want, Mistress. Anything at all."

"That's a dangerous word around here. Let's go find out what you mean by *anything*."

———

THE STORY CONTINUES in The Last Good Knight, *available now in a new Original Sinners Pulp Library mass-market paperback edition and ebook from 8th Circle Press.*

Tiffany Reisz is the *USA Today* bestselling author of the Romance Writers of America RITA®-winning Original Sinners series from Harlequin's Mira Books.

Her erotic fantasy *The Red*—the first entry in the Godwicks series, self-published under the banner 8th Circle Press—was named an NPR Best Book of the Year and a Goodreads Best Romance of the Month.

Tiffany lives in Kentucky with her husband, author Andrew Shaffer, and two cats. The cats are not writers.

Subscribe to the Tiffany Reisz email newsletter:

www.tiffanyreisz.com/mailing-list

www.ingramcontent.com/pod-product-compliance
Lightning Source LLC
Chambersburg PA
CBHW021124070726
47591CB00013B/794